The Big Test

the Big Test

Julie Danneberg

Illustrated by Judy Love

To my brothers: Dan, Ed, and Andy.
Thank you for your strength and presence
as we faced our own Big Test.
                                        —J. D.

For Roger, who has been there for me
from the first scribbled sketches through
the final scans. With gratitude and love.
                                        —J. L.

Published by Charlesbridge
85 Main Street
Watertown, MA 02472
(617) 926-0329
www.charlesbridge.com

Library of Congress Cataloging-in-Publication Data
Danneberg, Julie, 1958–
    The Big Test / Julie Danneberg ; illustrated by Judy Love.
        p. cm.
    Summary: Mrs. Hartwell is concerned that preparing her students to take the Big Test
is only making them nervous, and so she thinks of a way to help them relax.
    ISBN 978-1-58089-360-2 (reinforced for library use)
    ISBN 978-1-58089-361-9 (softcover)
[1. Examinations—Fiction. 2. Test anxiety—Fiction. 3. Teachers—Fiction. 4. Schools—
Fiction.] I. Love, Judith DuFour, ill. II. Title.
PZ7.D2327Big 2011
[E]—dc22   2010022762

Printed in China
(hc) 10 9 8 7 6 5 4 3 2 1
(sc) 10 9 8 7 6 5 4 3 2

Illustrations done in ink and transparent dyes on Arches watercolor paper
Display type hand-lettered by Judy Love and text type set in Electra
Color separations by Chroma Graphics, Singapore
Manufactured by Regent Publishing Services, Hong Kong
Printed November 2011 in Shenzhen, Guangdong, China
Production supervision by Brian G. Walker
Designed by Diane M. Earley

M rs. Hartwell felt good.
Really good.
Really, really good.

All year long her students had worked hard,
learned lots, and had fun.

And now, as the school year neared its end, Mrs. Hartwell told her students that they were ready to take the Big Test.

"Yuck," said Eddie.

"Double yuck," said Alexandra.

"Double, triple, quadruple yuck,"
said Josh. "I hate tests."

Mrs. Hartwell laughed. "Don't worry, this test is
just a chance to show how much you've learned."

"...e addition," Emily shouted out.

"And reading," said Maria.

"And science," Jack joined in.

Mrs. Hartwell nodded in agreement.

Leaning forward, she added, "We still have
one thing left to learn, though."
The class was confused.
"But you just said we were ready," Daniel said.

"You are. Almost. But o███████ou also have to
know
how to *show*
what you *know*,"
explained Mrs. Hartwell. "It's the last thing we
have to learn. It will be fun."

So during reading that morning, Mrs. Hartwell sent the students right to their seats. "Today we're going to practice our sitting-still-for-long-periods-of-time skill. I want you to read at your seat and work by yourself."

"That doesn't sound like fun to me," Eddie grumbled as he took out his book.

The class worked quietly. The reading part was easy. Sitting still without making a sound was hard. For Andy it was impossible.

During recess, while everyone else ran and played, Andy ran and played—and worried.

After recess Andy's stomach hurt. He asked to go to the nurse.

"Okay," said Mrs. Hartwell sadly, "but you'll be missing this afternoon's let's-all-read-the-directions lesson."

Andy didn't mind.

On Tuesday morning Mrs. Hartwell said, "Friday is the day of the Big Test. Since we don't want any bubble trouble when we take it, we're going to practice our fill-in-the-bubble skills."

Everyone worked hard. Everyone did just fine.
Everyone, that is, except Emily and Maria.

By the time they were done working, Emily had a headache, and Maria felt shivery all over. They asked to go to the nurse.

"Okay," said Mrs. Hartwell, looking concerned, "but you're going to miss our morning-of-the-test-nutrition lesson."

Emily and Maria took their pass and rushed out the door.

On Wednesday morning Mrs. Hartwell said,
"Today we're going to take a practice test."

"Do we have to sit still for long periods of time?" asked Andy.

"Yes," said Mrs. Hartwell.

"Do we have to fill in bubbles?" asked Emily.

"And be sure to follow the directions?" asked Maria.

"Yes, you do." Mrs. Hartwell smiled encouragingly. "Remember, this test is a chance to show what you know . . . before the timer goes off."

Although most of the class did just fine, by the time the practice test was over, Daniel had gone to the nurse.

As Mrs. Hartwell watched him go, she felt bad. Really bad. Really, really bad.

On Wednesday afternoon, just before the bell, Mrs. Hartwell reminded everyone that tomorrow was the last day before the Big Test.

"We know, we know," Eddie said grumpily. "This Big Test is no fun. I can't wait for it to be over."

All the other students nodded in agreement.

As Mrs. Hartwell straightened up her desk, she said, "Tomorrow will be better, I promise."

When the students entered the classroom on Thursday, Mrs. Hartwell greeted them with a smile.

"You've all worked hard this year, learned lots, and had fun, right?" she asked.

"Yeah," said the class.

"And this week we practiced how to show what you know, right?"

"Right," said the class hesitantly.

"Now it's time for the most important lesson of all," said Mrs. Hartwell.

The class groaned as she told everyone to line up.

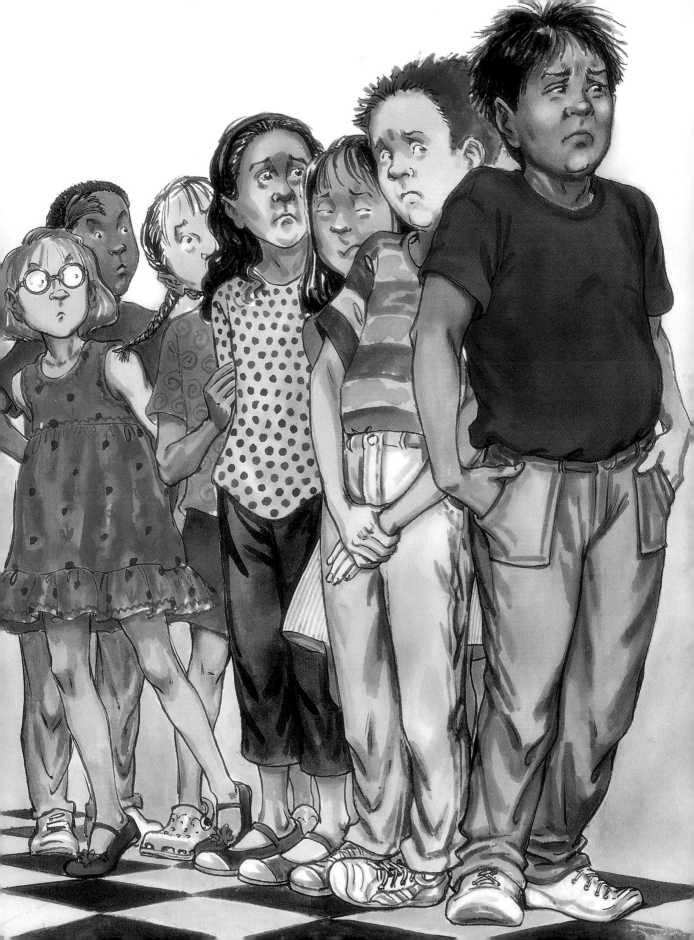

Mrs. Hartwell walked her students down the hall.
Everyone felt a little bit nervous.
Mrs. Hartwell walked her students right up
to the door of the library.
Everyone felt a *lot* nervous.

They gasped when she hung a sign
on the library door.
"I feel sick," said Eddie.

**LIBRARY
CLOSED**

STUDENTS TESTING

Mrs. Hartwell said, "Once you've
learned what you can learn and
know how to show what you know,
it's time to . . .

So the class did just that. And when the students finished the Big Test on Friday, they felt good.

Really good.

Really, really good.